Unintended Tales

Natalia Casali

Original stories written in Spanish
English versions by Isabel del Rio

The publication of these short stories has been possible thanks to those who have provided me the guidance and support to accomplish this goal. I am grateful to –

My mother and father for reading me tales with all their love and taking me to travel through imaginary worlds.

My husband, for offering his support from the beginning of my journey at writing.

My aunts Sandra and Marisol for encouraging me to keep writing.

Isabel Del Rio, for your guidance as my mentor, for sharing your talent as writer, always inspiring me to obtain the best results in my stories.

Dr Jennifer Langer and Dr David Clark, for their support and trust.

Lester G. Medina, friend and colleague, for his support from the beginning of the project.

For my father Ricardo,
and his intergalactic traveller soul

CONTENTS

Katyuska, The Soothsayer

Original story in Spanish: Natalia Casali. English version: Isabel del Rio

She had never resorted to magic spells or called on demons, nor had she ever engaged in the ritual killing of animals. Instead, she cleansed auras with the feathers of a Chaco eagle and burnt incense that she herself made from the flowers of the Guayabi tree. And on that particular afternoon, with the cicadas singing as persistently as always in such heat, Katyuska received a new visitor.

"So, you want to know whether this man is destined for you," she anticipated.

"Yes, that's why I'm here," the girl who had just arrived said. "Not knowing gives me so much heartache. At all times, he dwells within my innermost being and in my every thought. A sweet and good-natured man he is, in his prime and in the bloom of youth. But I can also sense other powers suggesting that our love isn't meant to be."

"So, are you ready?"

"I think I am, ma'am."

"Are you aware that all this could well be dangerous?"

"Really?"

"You see, child, you must be brave if you wish to find out what the Divine Spirit holds for you. And you'll only know through *Nalah*, the sun goddess."

"I was told that you'd be able to help me! They even said that you could make the most perilous quests come true! Taming rainbow boas and burrowing owls and..."

"That's how it is, child. Anything's possible when the warrior accepts the flow of *K'atá* as the Creator of all things and acknowledges the secrets of Time and Space."

Known as *La Rusa*, Katyuska Ivanov was one of the most famous soothsayers in Argentina. She was born in *Pampa del Infierno*, the Prairie of Hell, and had always lived in a town in Chaco Province. The daughter of Russian immigrants, she had gradually acquired the fine-looking features of the indigenous community in Qom. No one knew her age, but it was believed that she was anything between eighty and one hundred and twenty years old; and yet she looked as if she was barely over forty. Gossip had it that the father of her three children was a nocturnal sprite, a *Pombero*. And whenever she was expecting, the black-legged *Seriema* bird would settle on the roof of her house for three long days.

She was also skilled in the art of healing with plants and herbs, as well as with other mysterious preparations. Katyuska could read the shapes and contours that appeared on the gourd when drinking mate; and from the walk of the grey brocket, she could tell who would next visit her. Such were her powers that, just from the song of a lapwing, she knew the day and the time when someone would die. She never told them, naturally, to avoid causing distress. But still, she knew.

The heat in *Pampa del Infierno* was agonising. Temperatures would peak to 56 degrees in the shade, and the locals avoided leaving their houses in the afternoon. Hence, the streets in the town were completely empty at that hour.

But unlike everyone else, the Russian never slept a siesta. She barely needed a quarter of an hour's rest, sitting alongside her black holy tree, *Nawe Epaq*. It was known that she survived on roots and water; and when she fasted, she thrived on the energy from the sun.

Although Katyuska lived in a small town in *Pampa del Infierno*, her predictions and prophecies were so accurate that news of her powers were known throughout the land and beyond. Celebrities from Buenos Aires would make the return trip by plane, even if only to put an end to the doubts and worries in their lives. Groups of tourists of every nationality made a stop in *Pampa del Infierno* to pay her a visit. Even successful entrepreneurs from other countries travelled there with their own interpreters to find out what would become of their business interests. Famous international celebrities did not miss the chance either. One of the locals said that she saw Paul McCartney and his daughter Stella in February that year. Another said that Lady Gaga was having a salad in a nearby canteen, smiling happily after a session. There were also rumours that *La Rusa* had extended Mick Jagger's life by three decades.

"Did you bring everything I requested?" Katyuska asked.
    "Yes, I did," said the girl.
    "Every little thing that I told you to bring?"
    "Yes, they're all here. I brought every single thing."
    Soledad was a girl of about twenty and from the town. She thought herself in love with a local man, yet she was plagued by doubts. One night, when crossing a field by foot, she saw lights shining in the dark, just like a night-wanderer. It could only be a

bad omen.

"So, ma'am, what will the reading be?"

"Ah, child, we'll use the old as well as the new."

"The old and the new?"

"Yes, we'll start with an astrological synastry chart to analyse the like-mindedness between you two fledglings, your beloved and yourself. And also to find out the dynamics of a prospective relationship. And then..."

"And then what?"

"We'll move to the new: analysing protein-coding genes and their genotype, all 25,000 of them, to see whether there's a genetic compatibility."

"As complicated as all that?"

"All this will give us the answer to your question about the man you think you love."

The young woman hesitated.

"But there're signs that tell a different story. They seem to be saying that we aren't meant for each other."

"What kind of signs?"

"In my dreams..."

"I see. Well, let's start with the cards to find out what the bridge of the subconscious shows us, and what symbols to look out for. The yellow-breasted crake on this particular card may not only reveal deluges and storms."

Katyuska took out her tarot cards and shuffled them. They were indeed dazzling cards, designed for her by the famed artist Roberto Miu Mau from Santiago, well-known for his portrayal of animals of every species.

The soothsayer placed three of those precious cards on the table. The one with forest cottontails depicted the lovers; a night monkey hanging from a tree portrayed a hangman; a red brocket with a machete symbolised death.

"Heavens! It's so clear what these depicted animals are saying. The cards never get it wrong," said *La Rusa*.

"That's what they told me about your card reading…"

" I don't want you to be frightened."

"Not even a werewolf can frighten me now!"

"I've a feeling that you already predicted what was going to appear on the cards."

"Yes, I anticipated much of what's here."

"Aye, and I can just about guess the man's name."

"Oh, don't say it out loud, I beg you! Walls have ears in this town!"

"Don't you worry, child."

"You see, it's as if I've lost my compass and I don't know where my rightful place is. I've never felt like this before. I dream of him constantly and, at the same time, I don't truly wish to be with him. In my dreams, he ends up vanishing just like that… sometimes because of the might of wind, and sometimes because of the flight of a dove."

"So, the man fades from your dreams?"

"Yes, that's how it is. But I've other dreams that are probably so much more significant. The other night I dreamt about a lapwing that could speak. And it would say things like: this is the way, you'll understand all this soon enough. And then I'd fly alongside the bird until we reached a stream."

"And what did you see reflected on the stream?"

"You, ma'am, appeared when I looked into the water."

"I understand."

"Ma'am, forgive me for being so inquisitive, but I'd like to know how much all this is going to cost me."

"Nothing at all! I won't charge you a dime. And that's because I don't really have any needs."

"I'd give you everything I own, but I've only got my dreams. That's all I have. I'm so grateful to you!"

Katyuska liked helping others without asking for anything in return. But people were so contented with her predictions that they provided her with generous donations: from large sums of money to expensive cars and properties. They say that Madonna bequeathed her a house in Miami and that Bill Gates presented her with one of the islands in The Maldives. But *La Rusa* never visited the house, nor did she ever fly to those islands. With the riches she received, she created schools for children and fed those in need. But she also used the funds to update her tools, so that she had at her disposal both the traditional methods of seeing the future and the latest technology that revealed everything there was to know about a human being.

"My child, come and sit here, don't you worry,' she said, and patted Soledad's hands softly.

"I'm not sure whether... whether I'm meant to be with this man. Last night, when I was thinking about him, an owl landed on my window and a mirror fell from the wall and shattered into a thousand pieces."

"Do you realise, child, that all these things you're telling me appear to be signs from *Nowet*, the lord of all Nature and all animals?"

"*Nowet?*"

"Yes."

"I feel... I feel as if I already knew all this."

"That is so."

"And how is it, ma'am, that you've such gifts?"

Katyuska never once thought that her gifts belonged to her. When she was asked, she would claim that she was filled with prodigious strength when helping others in their plight. It was said that her prowess began at a very young age. It happened when her father was caught under a tractor ploughing a field. Katyuska saw the accident happen as she was looking from the house where she lived with her parents. She had not yet learnt to speak but, at that moment, she began to sing a mysterious melody as the clouds concealed the sun. Within seconds, a beam from the heavens lifted the vehicle above the ground, and her father escaped unharmed. The beam then lowered the tractor, and the child Katyuska ended her song and smiled.

People also spoke about the only journey she ever made outside *Pampa del Infierno*. One day, she heard a strange and trembling voice that told her to set off on a journey. *La Rusa* left the following morning at dawn, with nothing but the clothes she was wearing and a rucksack containing plant roots and two litres of water. She crossed the Chaco by foot; she bordered part of Cordoba; and in Mendoza, she stopped to replenish her supply of water. She eventually arrived at Paso de Indios, in Chubut. She then realised that she had walked for twenty-one days without rest. Finally, she reached a small hut beside a cliff, where a Mapuche Indian was waiting for her. He was about to die, he announced. And he explained that he had called out to her through *Lalat*, the wind.

"I need to pass on to you the teachings of *Wallontu Mapu*, the Universal Space and all its Dimensions..."

"Here in my bag, I've got what you asked for, ma'am."

"So, you've brought a strand of his hair."

"I brought two, just in case."

"And a sample of his saliva?"

"Here's the gourd he uses to drink his *mate*."

"That's too bad. The poor guy will sure miss his gourd!"

"No, ma'am, it's mine – we drink *mate* together, he and I."

"Well, let's check the genetics now. There's so much here for us to see. Don't forget that the human genome, child, occupies more space than we can imagine. Over the years, I've acquired high-powered equipment that allows me to find out not only about the soul of those who come to see me, but also about their biological being. Out of sheer curiosity, you could say."

An incandescent tungsten light emerged from a metal cabinet beside the wall. Katyuska placed a strand of hair in one of the compartments, and the gourd in the other. She closed the flap and pressed a blue button.

"Let's have a look at the genes, child. All the regulatory sequences and other non-coding DNA. And with your permission, there's something I need."

"You've my permission, of course."

Katyuska pulled a strand of hair from Soledad and placed it inside a test tube. And then she took a swab from the inside of her mouth and positioned it beside the strand of hair. And finally, opening another door of that same cabinet, she pressed a red button.

"Don't get carried away by what you see, because there's no stronger force than the will of *Lik Aqte*. It's the heart that gives us life as well as the source of everything around us. What we, as humans, may create ourselves can never be the same as *Daní*, the Divine Power."

"And so, what happens now?"

"Thousands of genetic mutations will be analysed, both of yourself and your man. Let's get Science to work."

Soledad waited anxiously for the results. Her gaze seemed to be lost, as if calmly anticipating what she would be told. Katyuska drew the curtains until the room was almost dark, and from a chest of drawers she took out a tablet with a keyboard and a screen. She pressed a yellow button and asked Soledad for her date of birth. Typing it on the screen, she proceeded to wait.

Soon enough, a holographic image of constellations materialised. With her left hand, Katyuska shifted the stars until something caught her eye. With her index finger and her thumb, she zoomed in.

"All this is exhilarating, child!" she said, putting the gadget away.

A loud buzzer rang out, making the whole floor vibrate. It was followed by the sound of a printer. The task of those two machines was coming to an end. The young girl anxiously looked at Katyuska, knowing that the results were about to be announced. After reading almost a metre of printed paper, the soothsayer lifted her head.

"The mountain will race to quench the warrior's uncertainties, for the fruit is only to be found in the thirst of fighters. Rivers of copper will appear at dawn, but only when the soul is ready."

Katyuska's words did not startle Soledad, nor did they seem new in her eyes.

"The constellations shall be fused to the soul, and they shall all thus unite. Courage is to be found in the heartbeat of the grey brocket, so that my predictions may be deciphered."

Katyuska continued to explain what she had just found out, but Soledad could not hear her voice anymore. As her perceptions about the world began to change, she saw only the new around her. And when the lapwing flew towards the house and sat on the windowsill, it was as if everything had acquired a different dimension.

From the moment of her arrival, Soledad had noticed the vibrations of flowers swelling around the building, and their murmurs above the roof. And upon her skin she was able to sense the screeching of the walls as they warmed up under the sun, as well as the insistent cry of the cicadas.

The lapwing sang twice, perched as it was on the window. Yes, the lapwing sang. And then Soledad, as if she had anticipated it all, suddenly felt that she was in the forest. Her legs were yellow-coloured with black spots, and she saw herself running along the ground; and in her flesh, she experienced the texture of the earth and the swaying of the grass; she galloped on her four legs and yet she did not become tired; she could run, yes, just like a jaguar; and she could run so very fast because that is what she was. And she dragged her body close to the ground until she reached a tree and then began to climb, clambering with her little hairy hands that would hook onto the bark to help her get to the top; and she realised that she could jump from branch to branch, just like a howler monkey, because that is what she was. And when she had reached the highest shoot of tender leaves, she felt that she was leaving the tree behind; yes, she was travelling alongside the breeze, and she saw that her two wings were flapping; she felt the bursts of wind and the intensity of the heat in the haze surrounding her; and she looked down, and far away, below her, was a forest that pulsated along those sacred lands; and she flew like a red eagle, because that is what she was. She was no longer who she had been, for she could now be all things at once. And through the eyes of the soothsayer, she could see herself, at all times and in all dimensions. Her freshly found perceptions gave new and unknown contours to what surrounded her, and stillness prevailed within her. She then thanked all those fortuitous signs that she had previously foreseen. But most of all she thanked the platonic form of love that she had experienced and that, nurtured solely on the mundane, had sparked moments of a divine and perfect nature.

The shrill of the cicadas had turned into the singing of celestial beings. And that was when Soledad felt close to the soul of the tree of *Nawe Epak* and all other trees; and comprehended that she could embrace them all at once, in all their dimensions. And then she heard the invocations of all creatures, both their laughter and their laments. And as her affection towards all things spread and became everlasting, she produced an infinite sigh of yearning.

The streets were still silent and empty in the afternoon heat. Only the lapwing was about to be heard again. Yet Soledad already knew that the bird would sing. She knew everything that was about to happen, and everything that had already happened, for it was all taking place at the same time. She also knew why she was there, but then she had always known it. Even before the lapwing sang, and even before that, she knew. And just as lightning can appear without warning, she knew what was going to happen next: Katyuska was about to die. Or was about to change shape and acquire a new form, which was the same thing. And Soledad would have to remain there, in that house, taking the place of the soothsayer and fulfilling her calling, although she had always done so because she had always known it.

Katyuska saw for herself the visions appearing in Soledad's eyes.

"Now that you've heard the beating heart of *Lik Aqte*, you'll experience the Divine Dichotomy, and you'll be one with the will of the Supreme *K'atá*."

The lapwing took off from the window. Katyuska witnessed it and smiled.

"Before I leave, my child, I'd like to celebrate with you by drinking *mate*."

The Shadow

Original story in Spanish: Natalia Casali. English version: Isabel del Rio

The criminal case against Katryna Bielecki was taking much longer than usual. With the deadline to submit supporting documents about to expire, we had to act fast. We certainly needed as much incriminating evidence as we could get our hands on. I'd already been working for six months in the firm, and although my probation period was over, I had to prove myself by winning significant cases. All of this meant that I had to work well over ten hours a day, and on weekends I had to work from home.

"Come on, Joanna, don't be such a sucker. You know you need to relax," said my colleague Barbara. "You can't spend the entire day in the office. You'll get ill!"

"I understand what you're saying, but it'll all be over soon."

"Why don't you continue with all this tomorrow. And now let's go and have a drink."

I didn't really want to go with her. I needed to stay in the office and check some new bits of evidence that had just arrived. And I had to get on with another case for a new client.

At that particular time, the pub was crammed. Barbara performed some kind of superhuman feat to cut through the crowd and get our beers.

"These stupid bartenders," she complained. "If only they'd rearranged the tables, there'd be more space for all of us standing here."

I stopped listening to her the moment I saw Julio. I pretended not to notice him, but I couldn't stop admiring his dark wavy hair; his large eyes, which seemed to be bathed in light; his particular way of smiling. Luckily my boss wasn't there, so we could have a nice long chat. I'd seen him in the pub before, but we'd never actually spoken. It felt as if I'd always known him. He approached me casually and asked me how everything was going at work. He was also a lawyer, a criminal lawyer, and he worked for a law firm located quite close to where mine was. The thing is that I wanted to be with him, but I couldn't stop obsessing about work: I was regretting not having checked the evidence that we'd received that morning and, even worse, not having prepared for the meeting with the new client. I told him that everything was fine and that I was happy with the cases I was dealing with. That sort of small talk, not much more. But I felt I was wasting my time, and I couldn't stay any longer. I just couldn't afford to.

"If you'll excuse me," I said to him. "I need to get back to my work in the office."

"What a shame!"

"Yeah, I know. But I need to work like mad these days."

"Don't worry, Joanna. Last week I was in the same boat as you, overloaded with work."

"Great! We can catch up next week."

He smiled, though he didn't look too happy. But I had to go. Yes, leaving the pub was possibly a mistake. I had a feeling Julio liked me, but I didn't stay to find out. There wasn't even time to give him my number. Perhaps nothing could have changed what happened that evening.

I wasn't planning to go to bed too late, so the moment I arrived home I sat at the kitchen table and began to work, as I usually did. I'd been sent copies of fake receipts and various emails, and immediately realised that the case was going to be complicated. We still didn't have sufficient grounds to charge Katryna Bielecki. I'd returned home for nothing, and I should've stayed in the pub with Julio. How I wished that I was at a different stage in my life, with a more settled job. And then I could perhaps think of starting a relationship. Apparently, Julio was always asking Barbara about me and my work, and he was probably interested in me. But then I couldn't possibly juggle so many things. To make matters worse, my boss knew him. I really wouldn't be able to dedicate the necessary time to a relationship, so it would turn out to be yet another failed liaison. The main thing now was to commit fully to my job. If anything, I wanted even more responsibility at work.

It was then that I noticed something moving along the wall. I thought I was being silly and that I'd freaked out because of my own imaginings. It was my shadow.

Receipts, payments to third parties, expenses, incriminating evidence. My mind was going around in circles, working at full blast. It was obvious that I didn't have enough evidence. It would certainly be a legal risk for my firm if I wasn't up to it in court, or if I couldn't convince the judge with the contextual information I had. The worst thing was that the sentence could well lead to a counterclaim by the defendant.

And then I saw the shadow again. It moved along the wall as if it had a life of its own. I stood very still to have a good look. It was now darker and denser than before. Or it was possibly a gust of wind blowing through the half-open window and making the lamp swing from side to side. I gave no more thought to the matter, although the shadow did seem to be getting larger and to be moving again.

"That beer I drank didn't agree with me, did it?" I thought.

And out of the blue, the shadow began to dance. It raised its arms and moved its hips. I looked behind me in case there was someone else there. But I was on my own. Yes, that was it; someone had spiked my drink.

"I'm imagining all this!"

As if it were responding to my comment, the shadow stopped dancing and put her arms akimbo. It shook its head as if saying no, over and over again. Surely, I was delirious. Not for a second could I believe what was happening, and I carried on with my work. Yet from the corner of my eye, I could see that the shadow had stopped moving its head. And when I looked in its direction, it stuck its middle finger at me.

"I must be incredibly stressed to believe that something like this can really be happening!" I said to myself.

Keeping an eye on the shadow, I switched off the light. The table was pushed noiselessly against me, and I fell on the floor. When I switched the light back on, I saw that the table had moved and that there was no reflection on the wall. The shadow had gone. My shadow. I began to look for it, at the same time trying to prove that it was all in my mind. But almost immediately I saw someone running along the corridor. It had switched on the light in the bathroom, and water was flowing from the tap. Whoever it was, it was hastily brushing its teeth. And then I heard the sound from my atomiser. Yes, someone was using it. I couldn't believe this was real: a shadow trying to spray my perfume on itself.

I went back to the kitchen and switched off the light both there and in the corridor. Everything was dark. Even the bathroom light was switched off. I quickly switched it back on to see whether the shadow was there, and sure enough it was. My shadow. It was quite still, there in the corridor. I'd exposed it finally. It didn't move, but it seemed to be separate from me. Independent of me, a distinct entity, acquiring volume as if filling up. It was also turning so much darker. The opaque darkness of its surface did not project any light, though its face had two shining spots. Yes, it had developed eyes.

We were both very still, opposite each other. Neither the shadow nor I were moving. Its newly acquired eyes were staring at me defiantly. I switched off the light, and the floorboards creaked. The shadow was moving. I switched the light back on, and it was in the middle of the corridor, even closer to me. I was terrified. It looked like some kind of opaque ghost, or even worse: the outline of something that had ceased to exist.

Again, I switched off the light, thinking that the vision would disappear forever. But in the darkness, I felt its quick footsteps retreat and I smelled the whiff of perfume. The shadow ran until it came to a halt. I then heard glass cracking and shattering, making a terrible noise. The shadow had broken one of the windows and had managed to jump outside. I lowered the shutters to stop anyone entering. And when I went to ensure the outside door was closed, I realised that the shadow had taken the keys.

"This cannot be happening", I said. "Yes, some hoaxer must have spiked my beer. The case is closed!"

And I went to bed.

Katryna Bielecki had worked for ten years as an accountant for ECOR, the gas provider. Within a few months of working there, she realised that no one ever supervised her work, and so she spent the following nine years falsifying invoices as well as every single receipt. It is believed that she made some $150,000 over that period, but it could have been more. The Human Resources Department was carrying out an internal investigation, and they suspected that she had accomplices within the company. They had searched her flat and found a pen drive with copies of documents, overpaid tax demands and duplicates of claims that had already been dealt with. My job was to represent the company.

I felt exhausted after the previous night, but I had to speak to the client. I asked Barbara to read the report and check for errors.

"Girl, you've got great big bags under your eyes!" she said. "You're the queen of jerks. And you should've bedded Julio. When you left the other day, he kept gazing at the door of the pub for quite a while. Just like a dog waiting for its master. So ridiculous! Once you left, that was the end of that!"

"Yes, I know," I said.

It was true; massive bags showed under my eyes. I hadn't slept a wink, and at five in the morning I had jumped from my bed because it sounded like someone was beating pots and pans in the corridor. And then I remembered my paranoia from the night before and the incident with the shadow. I wanted to go back to sleep, but I had to find out whether there was any truth in all this, or whether it was solely my mind playing tricks.

The kitchen was a mess. Beer cans, cigarette butts, bottles of my best whisky on the worktop. The keys beside the door. The damned window, completely smashed. Yes, it was all true.

I went to the sitting room, and I finally saw it. There it was: a woman, an opaque woman. What had previously been my shadow was now a woman, sleeping peacefully on my sofa. Her mouth was half-open, and she was softly snoring.

"What are you doing here?" I shouted. "Have you seen the mess you left in the kitchen?"

She made a dismissive sign with her hand.

"You've no idea what's awaiting you!" I threatened.

I took a deep breath and prepared myself a soothing cup of linden tea. All this can't be real, I thought, I must be under the effect of something, and all this is nothing but the product of my imagination. But what if it wasn't? I had to have a plan in place. I couldn't very well report my shadow to the police. If all this came to light, I could lose my job and my career would be ruined. Even if it was some kind of delirium, I needed to leave and go to the office. But before leaving, I had to stop that vile woman from doing whatever she felt like doing in my house. The best thing would be to lock her up in the laundry room. It had no window, so there'd be no escaping. I had to fool her somehow because there was no way I'd be able to force her into that room. I then thought about chocolate muffins. She was part of me, so she had to have similar likes and preferences. I woke her up and showed her a couple of muffins.

The shadow did not move. She was reeking of drink, totally drunk. After a few minutes, I woke her up and showed her the muffins.

"Look! There aren't too many muffins left. If you don't eat them, I'll eat them myself. And the bad news is that they're not selling this brand in the local supermarket anymore."

Making a huge effort, she managed to stand up and, staggering like a drunkard, she followed me to the laundry room.

"Come in, my sweet," I said. "Feel at home!"

I left the muffins inside and, pushing the door against her with all my might, I managed to lock it. With some luck, she'd fall asleep and stay there until I got home. I took a sedative and left for the office.

The clients had called and said they'd be there in the afternoon to deliver the pen drive.

"Our boss is going to be blockhead of the year!" Barbara said. "He comes over, he looks worryingly at you, and then he leaves. He's done that three times today."

"Really?"

"You're not delayed with the Katryna case, are you?"

"No, certainly not."

"By the way, I've learnt that her counsel has resigned. So now she has no one to represent her."

I thought that perhaps my boss was aware of what had happened. He never missed a thing in the office. Maybe he'd noticed that I didn't have a shadow any longer but decided to keep quiet. Thank goodness, he hadn't mentioned it. But was all this also on my mind? Did anyone else apart from me know about my shadow having a life of its own?

It was still five o'clock and I couldn't concentrate on my work. I wouldn't stop thinking about what I'd gone through. I wondered whether that opaque woman was still locked up in the laundry room. The door didn't shut so well, and she'd probably trashed the door as she'd done with the window. The window! I'd forgotten about it. I immediately called the insurance company. At work, I explained that a window in my flat needed repairing and I promised to work overtime the next day to make up for it. So, I went back home.

The door to the laundry room had been completely wrecked. The sitting-room was in a total state of disarray. The sofa was strewn with food, and empty beer cans adorned the shelves. The shadow now seemed to be swigging the vodka.

Yes, there she was, with the music playing full blast. She was dancing on her own, the tramp, as if in the middle of a dance floor.

"Are you mad?" I said and turned off the music. "Tomorrow I'll start a case against you, whoever you may be. And if you don't leave immediately, you'll end up living the rest of your bleeding life behind bars."

She turned towards me, her face consumed with hatred. She then ran along the corridor, chucking everything she could find on to the floor. She ended up in the bathroom, sprayed some of my perfume and again jumped out of the broken window.

"Don't you ever dare return, you bitch!"

Hell, she had taken the keys to the house again.

"Is everything alright, lady?" the builders, who'd come to repair the window, asked.

"Did you see that?"

"Something seemed to move, it all happened very quickly," said one of them.

"It was like a huge black cat," said the other.

This was a good sign. Both workmen had seen it. It wasn't all in my mind.

Once the window was repaired, I cleaned up the terrible mess she'd left behind. And then I realised what the time was. Ten o'clock at night. I sat waiting for her. But I was so tired that I couldn't keep my eyes open and I ended up falling asleep, which proved to be a huge mistake.

"Come on, girl, come on!" I heard someone shout.

I checked the time. It was three o'clock in the morning.

"Come on!" said a man's voice.

Yes, there was a man in my house. And I could also hear a banging sound. The outside door was open, and I locked it. I walked along the corridor towards the bedroom.

"Yes, girl, you're doing great!" shouted the man.

I was now in my bedroom. The bed was hitting the wall. And as I approached, I could hear the same voice.

"Come on, girl!"

As I pushed open the door, I saw them. Both of them. I couldn't believe what I was seeing. There she was, the shadow, having sex with a man. He was behind her. Both of them very focussed on what they were doing. And something was familiar. The man was him.

"It's you!" I said.

"Joanna?"

"I can't believe it!"

"What are you doing here?"

"What do you mean?"

It was Julio, the guy I liked. I couldn't understand how and where she'd found him.

"Enough! Get out of here, both of you!"

He seemed shocked, covering his nakedness with the sheets. She didn't move but only turned her head towards me. She gave me the finger as she always did.

"Get out!" I said.

Julio looked at me in disbelief.

"What are you doing here, Joanna?"

"What do you mean? This is my house! Get out of here both of you, or I'll call the police!!"

"I'm sorry, I didn't know this was where you lived. The girl told me that she lived on her own."

"How on earth could she have told you that? She can't speak!"

"She led me to believe that..."

"I'm calling the police right now. And I'll accuse you of breaking into my property. A case of forced entry!"

He nodded and got dressed in front of both of us. That's when I realised that I'd been a sucker. I should've returned home with him on that fateful night, and this rotten woman would have remained in her place like the shadow that she was. My shadow.

I accompanied Julio to the door.

"Is the girl your sister? Or is it that you grew up together?"

"No, that's not it at all!"

"It's bizarre. It's like she's got your same essence..."

"Really?"

"Well, she's a bit wilder than you."

"She's my wretched shadow!" I shouted.

"Your shadow?"

"Goodbye, Julio," I said, and shut the door.

Back inside, my shadow was sitting on the floor, crying without making a sound. She looked like a child, and I felt sorry for her.

"If you wish, you can still see Julio. But don't you dare bring him here. You know how much I liked him, and what you did was to take him from me."

I helped her to get up, but she pushed me away. She produced some kind of muted scream and got on her feet, throwing books and various items to the floor. She broke the lamp into smithereens, as well as all of my framed pictures. And as if that wasn't enough, she viciously kicked the furniture.

She was trashing everything, so I pulled her by her hair and pushed her. She was now lying on the floor and my hands went to her neck. She fought back, hitting and kicking me, but I pressed as hard as I could even violently, using all my strength. I didn't know what I was doing. But she wouldn't stop moving, so I wrung her neck with even more force. It was either her or me. My shadow or me. She was taking over my life and would end up ruining me. I went on squeezing and twisting her neck; I can't say for how long. I was beside myself and continued to press until she stopped moving. She finally collapsed, flopping like a little bird. Nothing glowed on her face; her eyes were now closed. I stood back and looked at her. She was fading away; in that state, she didn't seem capable of any malice or mischief. And again, I felt so sorry for her.

Time froze. I thought I would go mad after what had taken place. I tried to revive her, but she would not move. Nothing, not a whimper, not a sigh. Her opaqueness became translucent, and she gradually deflated. A shadow losing its volume...

I wanted to make everything go back to what it was. And so to stop the shadow from escaping again, I tried to attach her to my body, but she was so flimsy that she wouldn't cling to me. I tried to sew her to my clothes, yet the thread wouldn't hold her in place. Her body had now turned into a piece of misty black velvet, like the intangible versatility of matter, and she seemed to dissolve between my fingers. And then I thought that a bath would revive her, but neither bath-salts nor soap lather had any effect. I sprayed starch on her and tried to iron her back to me, convinced that this would help to keep her firmer. But it was her strange destiny to remain as some kind of indeterminate substance. It was as if she could contain within herself the three states of matter...

I couldn't comprehend why I'd done what I did. In any case, what had I become? What would they do to me if they could prove that I'd mistreated my own shadow, that I'd tortured it and then killed it?

For culpable homicide, I would get from six months to three years in prison. And what if they considered that it was a case of aggravated homicide? The sentence would be anything between 15 and 22 years. The worst, of course, would be life imprisonment without any possibility of parole. I felt lost, I didn't know what to do. And without causing her any further injury, I left her lying on the bed and then proceeded to do something that she used to enjoy. I went out to get some chocolate muffins, which we both liked so much.

When I returned, she was no longer on the bed. Once again, the window had been broken.

The phone rang. It was Barbara.

"Hey, girl, where have you been? You know what? They've stripped you of all your cases. And they're saying that the Bielecki case has been seriously delayed because of you. That it's all your fault!"

"What do you mean?"

"Yes, girl, they've sacked you."

"I don't understand!"

"I bet it was the boss, that brute!"

"But why? It wasn't going so badly. Why?"

"I knew that he was going to play you a rough one!"

"But they can't get rid of me. They've got to explain. I can go on dealing with the case! I'll work overtime, with more commitment, more dedication!"

"I'll call you later. He's coming over to speak to me now."

I took a taxi and went over to my office. When I arrived, I saw my boss talking to my shadow. She was sitting in my chair, in front of my computer; he was smiling.

"You have a phenomenal CV," he said to her. "The job is yours!"

It was ten o'clock at night when I got home. I sat on the sofa, and I ate all the muffins that I'd bought that morning. Maybe the criminal case against Katryna Bielecki had made me lose my job, but I knew what was needed to win the case. It was just a matter of switching sides. My shadow didn't know what awaited her, but I certainly did.